Shop Till We Drop

Creepy Crawlies

Join the Creepy Crawlies in all their
fun-packed adventures!

 Be sure to read:

Home Sweet Home

The Talent Contest

... and lots, lots more!

Shop Till We Drop

Hat'o'RamA!

Tony Bradman
illustrated by Damon Burnard

For my own personal Imelda ... and her sister Louise, Queen of online shopping!

This edition produced for the Book People Ltd,
Hall Wood Avenue, Haydock, St Helens WA11 9UL

First published by Scholastic Ltd, 2005

Text copyright © Tony Bradman, 2005
Illustrations copyright © Damon Burnard, 2005

ISBN 0 439 95447 9

Printed and bound by Tien Wah Press Pte. Ltd, Singapore

The rights of Tony Bradman and Damon Burnard to be identified as the author
and illustrator of this work respectively have been asserted by them in
accordance with the Copyright, Designs and Patents Act, 1988.

Chapter One

In a corner of The Garden, beyond The Flower Bed and underneath The Big Bush, three little creatures were enjoying a quiet Saturday at home.

Lucy the Ladybird was watering her pot plants.

Billy the Beetle was working out on his rowing machine.

And Doug the Slug was doing what he did best – lying on the sofa watching TV.

Suddenly they heard a loud squealing,
and Imelda the Centipede, the fourth little
creature in the house,
came running
downstairs, waving a
magazine and rippling
with excitement.

"Look at this, everybody!" she said.

Lucy, Billy and Doug peered at the magazine. In it there was an article about The Big Bug Ball, an event taking place that evening at The Bug-O-Drome.

There would be fantastic food, dancing to top bands, and prizes to be won – including one for The Most Elegant Creepy Crawly at the Ball.

"I'd like to go too," said Doug. "The food sounds amazing!"

"You can count me in as well," said Billy.
"I love dancing!"

"We'll all go," said Lucy. "It'll be fun.
You're bound to win the prize for being the
most elegant creepy crawly, Imelda.
You always dress so nicely."

"Do you really think
so?" said Imelda,
her eyes glowing.

"Oh yes," said
Lucy. "You
certainly put
enough time into it..."

"I'd love to win," said Imelda. Then she stopped rippling and looked panic-stricken. "But I don't stand a chance, Lucy. My hair is a mess, and I don't have a thing to wear. I've changed my mind. I'm not going!"

"Okay," said Doug. "We'll tell you about it when we get home."

"Don't be silly, Imelda," said Lucy, giving Doug one of her glares. "You just don't have enough confidence in yourself, that's all. You'll be fine."

Imelda looked unsure.

"Besides," went on Lucy, "you've got the rest of the day to shop for a new outfit."

"That's true," Imelda murmured. "Wait a second – I can't possibly go shopping on my own."

"Ah, I had a lot planned for today…" said Lucy, who didn't like shopping.

Billy and Doug hated it. They had gone pale and were trying to sneak off.

But now Imelda seemed about to burst
into tears.

"Er … never mind," Lucy said quickly.
"Of course I will. You'll come too, boys –
won't you?"

Doug and Billy both froze in their tracks.
"Suppose so," they muttered.

Soon they were heading for The Garden
Mall, Imelda leading the way.

this wAy to
the GARdeN
MALL

Chapter Two

The Garden Mall was incredibly crowded and busy. The shops were packed with little creatures of every shape and size. And each of them seemed to be searching for a very special outfit with The Big Bug Ball in mind…

"Oh no," Doug groaned. "I don't think I'm going to enjoy this."

"Me neither," Billy murmured. "In fact, I'm fed up already."

"I bet I'm much more miserable than you," Doug whined.

"Oh, stop moaning, you two," Lucy snapped. "Hey, Imelda, wait for us!"

But Imelda was
a bug on a mission.
She dragged her
friends from
one shop …

to another …

and another…

She looked at hundreds of dresses and
bags, but nothing was right. And as for the
shoes … well, trying them on took for ever.

Lucy kept telling Imelda she looked great,
and Billy did, too. But all Doug did was
complain – except when he made fun of
the other shoppers.

"Hey, check out
that wasp," he
sniggered. "What
does she look like?"

Doug was staring at a large, over-dressed wasp hovering nearby. She had two fashion victim friends with her, a tiny bee and a long, thin grasshopper.

"I don't know," said Billy. "A wedding cake – or maybe a Christmas tree? It's strange, though – she and her friends seem to be everywhere we go…"

Eventually Imelda plunged into a shop called Frieda Fruit Fly's Fashion Frenzy. Lucy, Billy and Doug followed her. Imelda found an outfit she liked, and went to the changing room to try it on. Lucy and the boys waited.

Lucy didn't say a word. She just rolled her eyes and sighed.

"Are you ready?"
Imelda said at last.
"I'm coming out now!"

"Please let this be the one," Doug whispered. "Please, please…"

Imelda emerged in a wonderful outfit and stood before them, smiling shyly.

Suddenly the large wasp and her two
friends appeared. They hovered round
Imelda, buzzing and clicking and
looking her up and down.

"Oh, hi, Wendy, Brenda,
Glenda," said Imelda.
"Are you shopping
for the ball too?
What do you think
of this outfit?"

"Bad choice," said Glenda the Grasshopper.

That dress is hideous!

"It's so awful it's giving me a headache!" sneered Brenda the Bee.

"And those shoes!" screeched Glenda.

What can she be thinking!

"Well, it's obvious, isn't it?" said Brenda.

They match the bag!

They howled with laughter,
and Wendy the Wasp smirked.
"You're right, girls,"
she said. "It's the
worst outfit
I've ever
seen!"

Imelda stood there for a second, her
bottom lip quivering. Then she turned and
ran back into the changing room, sobbing
her heart out…

Chapter Three

"Imelda, are you okay?" said Lucy. There was no reply, only the sound of wailing behind the changing room doors.

Lucy turned on Wendy, Brenda and Glenda. "Who do you think you are? How dare you upset our friend like that! We thought she looked lovely, didn't we, boys?"

"Of course we did!" said Billy. He gave Doug a nudge.

"What?" said Doug. "Er, yeah … absolutely terrific!"

"Well, judging by the sad way you three are dressed, I hardly think your opinions count," said Wendy. Her chums tittered. "Come on, girls … mission accomplished, I think. Let's go and find ourselves some prize-winning outfits!"

With that, they swept out of the shop, giggling as they slipped into the crowd. Lucy stood watching them.

"What a cheek!" said Doug. "I don't dress badly, do I?"

"Quiet, Doug," said Lucy. "I'm trying to think. I'm sure those three didn't just happen to come along."

"No, you're right," said Billy. "They've been following us since we arrived at the mall. We've seen them lots, haven't we, Doug?"

Doug opened his mouth, but Lucy didn't give him a chance to speak.

"Following us, eh?" she murmured. "Well, Imelda obviously knows them. And what was all that mission accomplished stuff about?"

Billy and Doug glanced at each other, and shrugged. Suddenly the doors flew back, and Imelda emerged again.

"Ah, there you are, Imelda!" said Lucy.
"Listen, you shouldn't take any notice of
those three. You looked beautiful."

No, they were right.
I looked terrible...

"Well, er … what do you want to do?" said
Lucy. "We could keep looking. There must
be a couple of shops we haven't been to."

"Oh no," groaned Doug. "I was hoping
we could go home now."

"Don't be so selfish, Doug!" Lucy snapped.

"It's okay, Lucy," said Imelda, her voice shaking. "I want to go home too. I won't be going to the ball, so I won't need to do any more shopping … ever!"

She burst into tears and ran out of the shop, sobbing harder than before.

"Poor Imelda!" said Billy. "What shall we do now, Lucy?"

"You and Doug go after her and make sure she's all right," said Lucy.

I'll be home in a while...

Chapter Four

Lucy walked through the crowds in The Garden Mall, searching for Wendy, Brenda and Glenda. She heard them long before she saw them. They were sitting outside The Creepy Crawly Coffee Shop, talking very loudly.

Lucy sat at a table
behind a pillar,
ordered a coffee,
and listened.
What she heard
made her very cross.

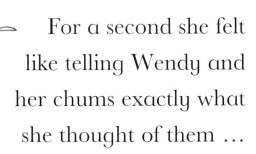

For a second she felt
like telling Wendy and
her chums exactly what
she thought of them …
but then she had a better idea.
She gulped down her coffee and hurried
home.

Things weren't going too well at the little house. As Lucy came up the path, she saw a huge heap of shoes in the front garden.

And as she walked up to the front door, several more pairs came flying out of an upstairs window.

Lucy ducked, and went inside.

Billy was waiting in the hall. "Oh, thank goodness you're back, Lucy!" he said, his eyes wide with worry. "Imelda's in a terrible state. She's locked herself in her room."

"She's been making a racket, too," said Doug. He was lying on the sofa in the front room.

Just at that moment there was a whole
series of BANGS! and CRASHES! above
their heads, followed by some loud
RIPPING and TEARING noises.

Lucy frowned, hurried upstairs, and
knocked on Imelda's door. "Imelda, I've
got something to tell you," she said. "About
Wendy."

Lucy had to knock several more times, but eventually Imelda opened the door. She had emptied her wardrobe, and torn apart most of her clothes.

"It was all a plot to stop you going to the ball, Imelda," Lucy explained. "I heard Wendy saying she wants to win the prize for being the most elegant creepy crawly, but she was sure you would because you always look fantastic!"

Imelda didn't look convinced. "Honestly," said Lucy. "She got her friends to say those things so you wouldn't go this evening."

"Really?" Imelda murmured. "She said I look fantastic?" Lucy nodded. "Okay, then," said Imelda, smiling. "I *will* go to the ball this evening."

Billy, Doug and Lucy smiled at one another.

"But no, I can't," Imelda wailed, her smile suddenly vanishing. "Now I really don't have a thing to wear … and it's too late to go back to the mall!"

"Step aside," said Lucy. Her patience had run out. "I'll find you something to put on. You're going to this ball even if I have to drag you there…"

Chapter Five

With Lucy's help, Imelda managed to assemble an outfit for the ball, although it was rather ripped and torn and, well … quite unusual. Although strangely enough, Imelda didn't seem to mind.

"You know, I've been thinking," she said
as the four of them left the house that
evening. "Maybe I do worry a little too
much about how I look…"

Doug snorted, and Billy struggled to keep
a straight face. "Oh, I don't think so," said
Lucy, glaring at the other two. But Imelda
wasn't listening.

"It's times like these that make you understand fashion isn't important," said Imelda. "What matters is your friends. And you three have been so nice to me today, I realize now how lucky I am. Who cares about Wendy and Brenda and Glenda and some stupid prize? Let's just enjoy ourselves!"

"Although I can't help wondering…" said Imelda. "Are you sure these colours work together? And I do have a few doubts about these earrings…"

"Imelda, you're impossible!" said Lucy. "Now come along, we're here…"

They hurried inside the Bug-O-Drome, where a fantastic sight greeted them. There were tables piled high with delicious food, a great band playing, and a vast crowd of happy little creatures having a wonderful time.

"Oh yeah, party ON!" yelled Doug, and headed straight for the food.

"Don't look now," muttered Billy, "but isn't that Wendy over there?"

Wendy, Brenda and Glenda were pointing at Imelda and sniggering.

"Ignore them," said Lucy, so that's what they did.

Doug spent the first hour at the food table trying every single thing. Then he found Lucy, Billy and Imelda, and the four friends danced the night away.

Finally it was the moment for all the prizes to be announced. The crowd of little creatures stood hushed as DJ Jazzy Jitterbug stepped on to the stage to read out the names.

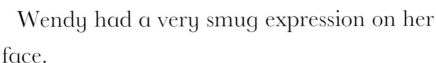

Wendy had a very smug expression on her face.

Billy was very disappointed not to win the prize for Best Dancer. "But it's not fair!" he muttered. "I was absolutely brilliant…"

"No, you weren't," giggled Doug, "you've got six left feet."

"Very funny," said Billy. "Well, they should have given you a prize for eating."

"Oh, for heaven's sake, you two," hissed Lucy. "Be quiet! He's about to announce the big prize."

Shhh!

"And last but not least," said DJ Jazzy Jitterbug, "the prize for The Most Elegant Creepy Crawly at the Ball goes to …"

Imelda! Great outfit, Imelda!

Wendy fainted. But Imelda squealed with delight, and went up to collect her prize – a cheque for a large amount of money … to spend on clothes!

LoAdsA money!

"Thank you, thank you!" said Imelda, crying. "I simply couldn't have done it without my three special friends, so I'll need their help to spend this…"

"Oh no…" Doug moaned. "You know what that means, don't you?"
"Yes, it looks like we're going to shop till we drop," Billy grumbled.

"Oh well, I can think of worse things than going shopping with Imelda," said Lucy. Doug and Billy gave her a look.

"Er … okay, I can't," she said.
The three of them burst into laughter…
And then they went to join their friend.